THIS WALKER BOOK BELONGS TO:

_____

_____

_____

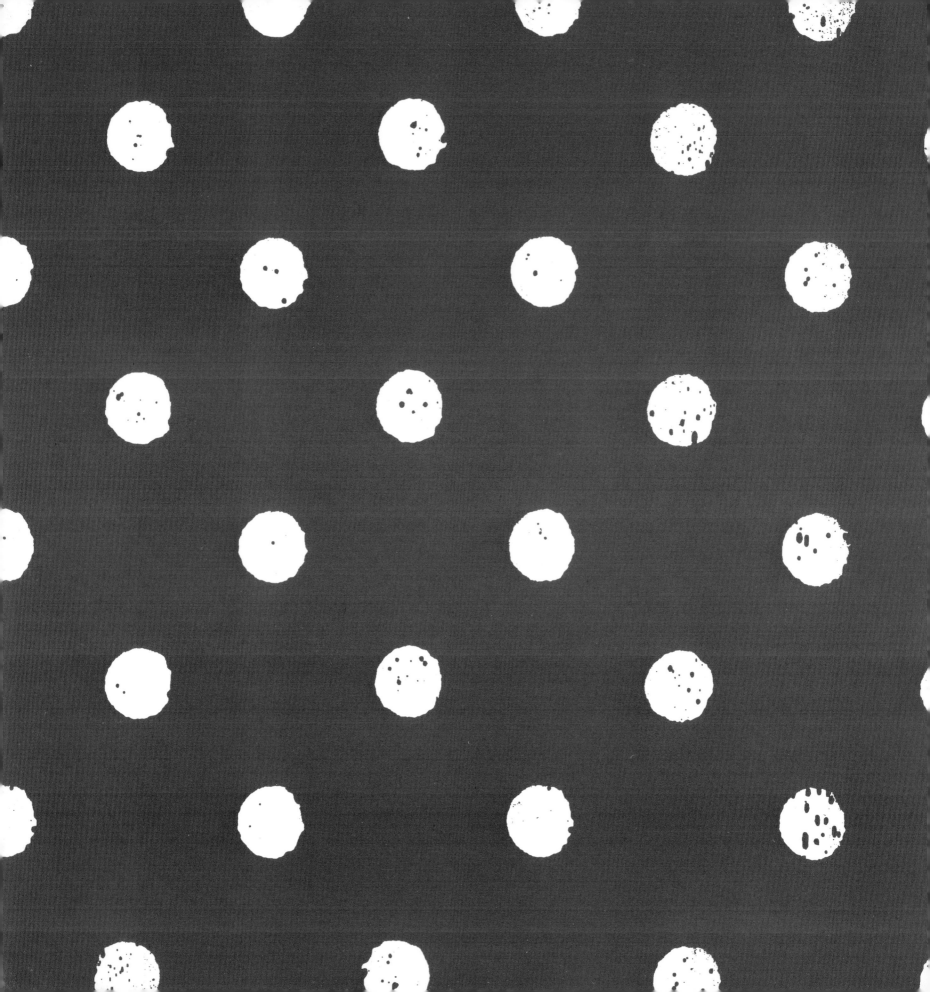

For Rocky Lawson,
the first pirate I ever met

First published 1994 by Walker Books Ltd
87 Vauxhall Walk, London SE11 5HJ
This edition published 2004
Reprinted 2004, 2005, 2006, 2007

© 1994 Colin McNaughton

The right of Colin McNaughton to be identified as
author/illustrator of this work has been asserted by him in
accordance with the Copyright, Designs and Patents Act 1988

This book has been typeset in PirateSchoolbook Roman

Printed in China

British Library Cataloguing in Publication Data:
a catalogue record for this book is available from the British Library

ISBN 978-0-7445-9896-4

www.walkerbooks.co.uk

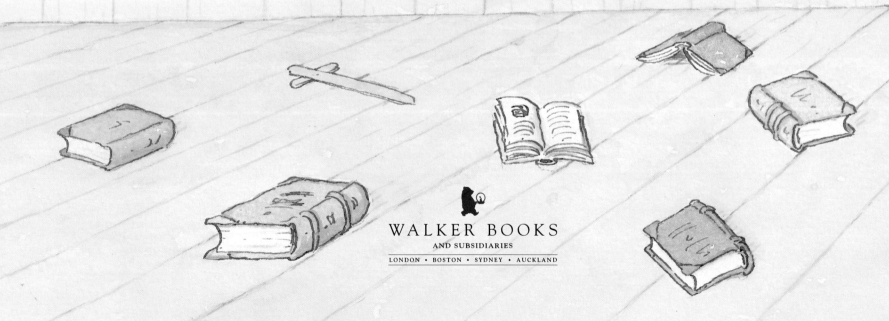

WALKER BOOKS
AND SUBSIDIARIES
LONDON · BOSTON · SYDNEY · AUCKLAND

CAPTAIN ABDUL'S PIRATE SCHOOL

COLIN McNAUGHTON

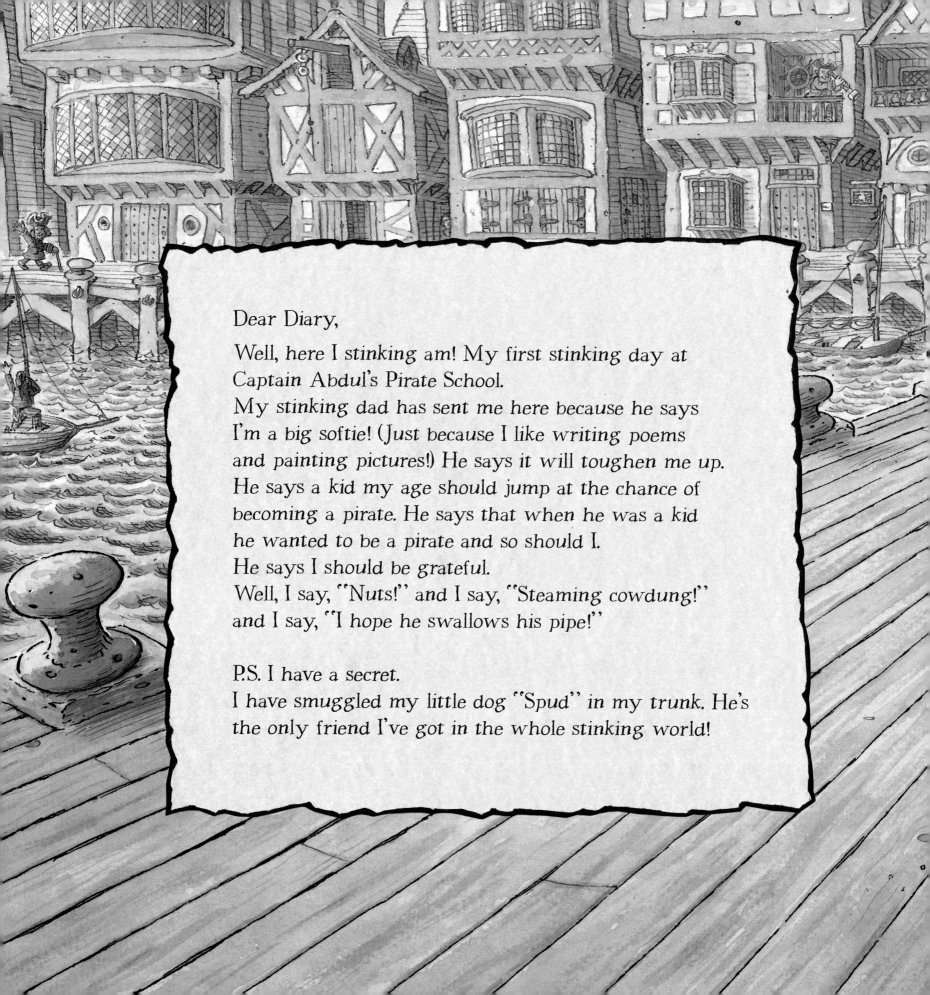

Dear Diary,

Well, here I stinking am! My first stinking day at
Captain Abdul's Pirate School.
My stinking dad has sent me here because he says
I'm a big softie! (Just because I like writing poems
and painting pictures!) He says it will toughen me up.
He says a kid my age should jump at the chance of
becoming a pirate. He says that when he was a kid
he wanted to be a pirate and so should I.
He says I should be grateful.
Well, I say, "Nuts!" and I say, "Steaming cowdung!"
and I say, "I hope he swallows his pipe!"

P.S. I have a secret.
I have smuggled my little dog "Spud" in my trunk. He's
the only friend I've got in the whole stinking world!

We were met at the door by Captain Abdul himself: hairy, scary and with more bits missing than a second-hand jigsaw.
"Follow me upstairs, me little buccaneers," said Captain Abdul, "an' we'll get yer kit stowed away, ooh-arrgh, that we will. Ha-har, ooh-arrgh!"

Hammocks ~ ooh ~ arrgh!

I was a bit *nervous* about meeting the other kids but they don't seem too bad – they look just as miserable as me. We then had supper and went to bed, where I wrote this and cried a bit for my mum.

Tom Tew

Anne Bonney

Simon Smee

Ben Gunn

Jack Rackam

Frankie Drake

Samuel P. Chop

Beryl Flynn

Mary Read

Bartholomew Sharp

Cc is for Cannon

Bb is for Bully

Ss is for Sword

Oo is for Ooh-arrgh

Hh is for Ha-har

Xx is for X marks the spot

Rr is for Rum

Tt is for Treasure

Aa is for Anchor

Dear Diary,

Woke up this morning and stood up in bed. Forgot I was in a hammock – bit of a headache. I was brushing my teeth when Bully-boy McCoy came in, "What yer doin' that for?" he asked. "If I don't, sir, my teeth will go black and fall out," I replied. "What's wrong with that?" he said. "Who ever heard of a pirate with nice teeth!" And he confiscated my toothbrush!

Today we studied history. Portobello Billy told us an exciting story about Calico Jack the pirate, set in his favourite place – the West Indies.

Dear Diary,

That beastly Captain Abdul has scolded me for being too neat and tidy. He suspects me of brushing my hair – "Combs an' hairbrushes, the possession of, is a floggin' offence, ooh–arrgh!" he told me.

Today we had arts and crafts. We learned how to make cannon balls, swords, fake money and how to put model ships into rum bottles. (Spanish Omar Lette very kindly emptied the bottles for us.)

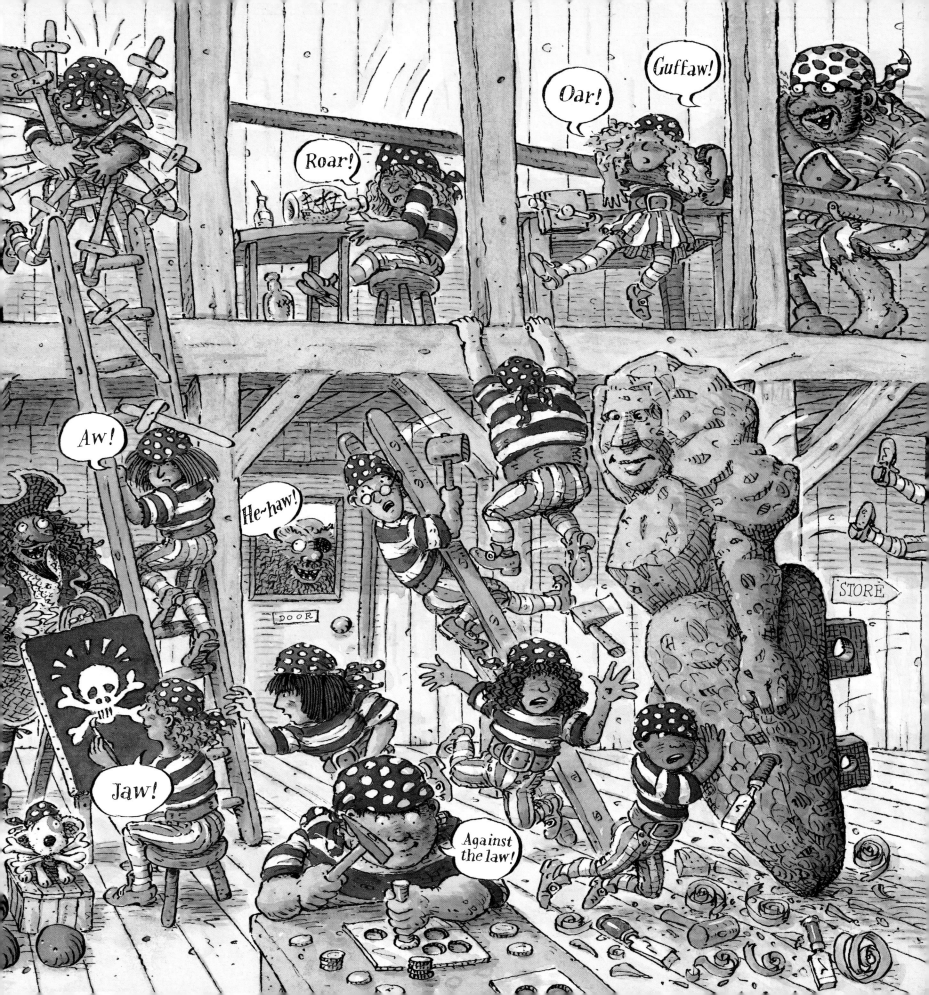

Dear Diary,

Last night we were doing our homework when Riff-raff Rafferty came in and caught little Simon Smee copying from another boy.

"Was you cheatin' boy?" howled Riff-raff.

"Yes, sir," said Simon Smee in a small voice.

"Good boy!" yelled the teacher. "Go to the top of the class!"

Today we learned how to speak pirate. Can't wait 'til next week's lesson. It's pirate swearwords! Ooh-arrgh!

Dear Diary,

The teachers had a party last night! They kept coming up and saying it was much too early to be in bed and why weren't we having a midnight feast or rampaging round the town looking for trouble! "Why, when I was your age," said the captain, "I already had a wooden leg! Ooh-arrgh!" When he finally woke up today he bellowed, "Fresh air is what we need, ooh-arrgh! We're goin' to sea!" For the rest of the day we sailed around the harbour in *The Golden Behind* learning pirate stuff.

Armed to the teeth with swords and ropes, our fearless band of pirate pupils crept down to the staff room. I gave the order and we attacked!

STAFF ROOM

Shhhh!

We rolled the teachers out on to the quayside.
"What *now*?" one of the kids shouted.
"We sail for the West Indies!" I cried. "Who's with me?
Who really wants to be a pirate?"
"ME! ME! ME!" they all shouted.
"Good!" said I. "Raid the kitchen, fill the water barrels
and get the ship ready. We sail in ten minutes!"
I wrote a note to our parents telling them what had
happened, pinned it to Captain Abdul, and we set sail.

Dear Diary, (six months later)

This is the life! We now call ourselves "Pirate pirates" because we only steal from other pirates. On our last raid we found out that pirates from all around the world had heard about our mutiny and, thinking how well taught we must have been, they have sent their kids to Captain Abdul's school! Abdul claims the mutiny was all his idea – part of his teaching plan. The scoundrel!

And so everybody is happy: Captain Abdul because his school is a roaring success; our parents because we send lots of treasure home; the kids because they get to sail and swim and fight and fire cannon and rob bullies and stay up all night.

And me? Well, I paint my pictures and write my poems and I'm captain of my own pirate ship! Who could ask for anything more...

I'm Captain Maisy Pickles – the happiest girl
in the whole, wide, wonderful world!

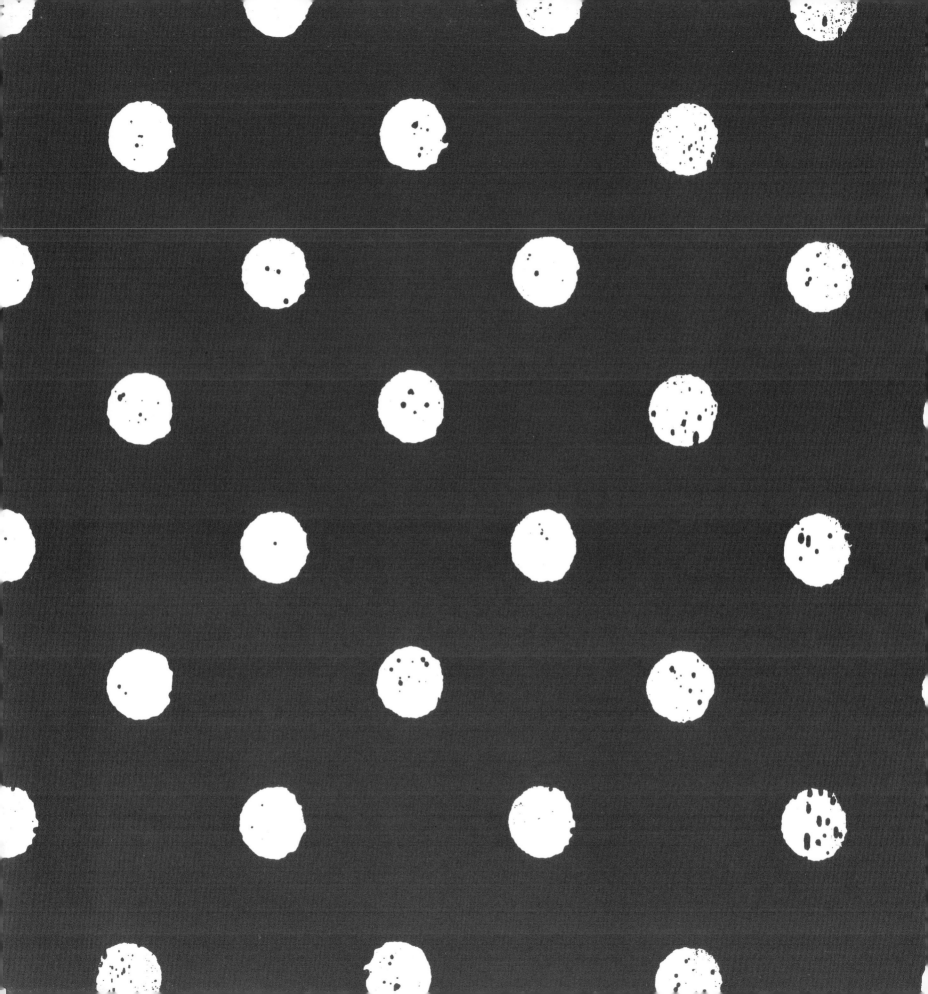

WALKER BOOKS BY COLIN MᶜNAUGHTON

★ Have You Seen Who's Just Moved In
Next Door To Us?
WINNER OF THE KURT MASCHLER AWARD

Making Friends With Frankenstein

Wish You Were Here
(And I Wasn't)

There's an Awful Lot of Weirdos
in Our Neighbourhood

Who's Been Sleeping in My Porridge?

I'm Talking Big!

When I Grow Up

Watch Out for the Giant-Killers!

Here Come the Aliens!

Who's That Banging on the Ceiling?

★ Jolly Roger
WINNER OF THE BRITISH BOOK AWARDS
CHILDREN'S BOOK OF THE YEAR AWARD

Captain Abdul's Pirate School

Captain Abdul's
Little Treasure

Potty Poo-Poo
Wee-Wee!

RED NOSE READERS *by* ALLAN AHLBERG
illustrated by COLIN MᶜNAUGHTON

Jumping • Push the Dog • Blow Me Down • Look out for the Seals
Tell Us A Story • Help • Me and My Friend • Bear's Birthday • Happy Worm
Shirley's Shops • Big Bad Pig • Fee Fi Fo Fum • Crash! Bang! Wallop!
One, Two, Flea! • So Can I • Make a Face